Paul's Adventures

WRITTEN BY JENNIFER HOLDER

ILLUSTRATED BY JOE BODDY

based on Acts 9, 16, 17, 23, 27, 28

Published by Standard Publishing, Cincinnati, Ohio
www.standardpub.com

ISBN 978-0-7847-2292-3

16 15 14 13 12 11 10 09 1 2 3 4 5

Standard®
PUBLISHING
Bringing The Word to Life

Cincinnati, Ohio

Slap, slap, slap. Saul's sandals slapped a rhythm on the road. He was on his way to Damascus to stop the Christians there from following Jesus.

Suddenly a bright light flashed in the sky and Saul was blinded. Saul fell to the ground. A voice said, "Saul, Saul, why are you hurting me?"

"Who are you?" Saul asked the voice. It was Jesus!

Led by his friends, Saul stumbled into the city.

Jesus told a man named Ananias to go to Saul. Ananias was afraid, but because he served Jesus, Ananias went anyway. Through God's power, Ananias healed Saul's eyes and helped Saul learn more about Jesus.

Now Saul loved Jesus. Saul wanted to please Jesus and be like him. Soon Saul became known to people as *Paul*.

Walk, walk, walk. Paul strode along the road once again. He traveled from city to city preaching the good news about Jesus. Paul told how Jesus had forgiven and changed him.

Many people who heard Paul's words became Christians. Wherever Paul went, churches began to grow.

In some towns, however, Paul's message made people angry. They accused Paul of stirring up trouble. The leaders in the town of Philippi decided to do something to stop Paul.

Scratch, scratch, scratch. Paul's feet scraped the floor as he was dragged through the door of a jailhouse!

Even though he was beaten and put in chains, Paul would not stop preaching and praising God.

Paul kept on walking from city to city. Paul preached, “Have faith in Jesus and your sins will be forgiven” and “You can live the right way with Jesus’ help.”

More churches began. But once again, some people became angry at Paul's words. One night, Paul made a narrow escape from the people who wanted to kill him! *Clop, clop, clop.* Horses' hooves quickly carried Paul away from the city of Jerusalem.

Paul's enemies—the people who hated to hear about Jesus—made more and more trouble for Paul. They did not want to change their wrong ways. The Roman officials did not know what to do about Paul. They arrested him.

Paul made another long trip. *Thunk, thunk, thunk.* Paul climbed the gangplank of a wooden ship headed to Rome.

Now a prisoner, Paul was unable to travel to the churches growing in faraway cities. But Paul still would not—*could* not—stop telling about Jesus.

Crunch, crunch, crunch. The feet that kicked up dust and gravel now belonged to a messenger. He was coming to get letters written by Paul to the churches.

We can read Paul's letters today! They make up a large part of the New Testament in the Bible.

Paul's letters say, "Be kind and compassionate to one another, forgiving each other, just as in Christ God forgave you" (Ephesians 4:32). "Stand firm in the faith; . . . be strong. Do everything in love" (1 Corinthians 16:13, 14).

Paul's letters can help us be better followers of Jesus. Now *we* can go and tell about Jesus. *Walk, walk, walk!*